NEVER Show a T-REX a Book

Rashmi Sirdeshpande & Diane Ewen

PUFFIN

NEVER
show a **T-Rex**
a book!

Just imagine if you do . . .

Well, she won't know what to do with it, will she?

She'll probably
think it's a hat.

Or a pillow.

Or a biscuit.

So you'll have to sit down and teach her how to read.

And if you teach her how to read . . .

. . . she'll get all excited and want to read even MORE.
So you'll have to sneak her into the library.

And if you take her
to the library . . .

PUBLIC
LIBRARY

CINEMA

. . . . she'll want to borrow
a lot of books.

A **LOT**
of books.

Books about space and pirates and jungles and dragons . . .
Books about cooking, books about music . . .

Books about numbers, and books about

fancy, complicated things that look VERY important.

And if you borrow ALL THOSE BOOKS . . .

. . . you'll have to hide
ALL of them
    AND the T-Rex
in your room
so your parents don't find out
or you'll be in
BIG trouble,
        won't you?

And when everyone's gone to sleep,
you'll have to sit up all night
reading with her . . .

And the next day you'll have to do it all over again.

And again.

And AGAIN!

Imagine that!

And if you read all those books . . .

. . . YOU are going
to get
very,
VERY
sleepy . . .

. . . and SHE is going to become very, **VERY** clever.

GRAND MASTER

MAKE THINGS DO STUFF

And if she becomes very, VERY clever, she might just decide that she's bored of just being a dinosaur.

She might decide that she'd prefer to be an artist . . .

a doctor . . .

a professor . . .

an architect . . .

a computer
scientist . . .

an astronaut . . .

or even . . .

. . . the PRIME MINISTER!

VOTE 4 T-REX

And if she becomes the Prime Minister, what do you suppose she'll do next?

The first thing she'll do is pass some new laws.
Everyone knows that dinosaurs LOVE watching films.
So she'll invite all her friends and make sure they have
bigger seats at the cinema.

And **bigger** tubs of popcorn!

Of course, she'll want to make sure that all her friends learn how to read too.
They probably won't all fit in your bedroom,

will they?

Imagine what will happen next!
You'll just have to take them to school with you.

That'll be · · ·
er · · ·

And if they all learn to read and all become really, really clever, there will be just no stopping them.

Can you
IMAGINE?!

ALL THAT
because you showed
a **T-Rex**
a book!

Right. That's quite enough
imagining for one day . . .

But there's nothing to stop you imagining
something **completely different** tomorrow!

This one is for all the LIBRARIANS out there.
You are WONDERFUL!
R.S.

For Maisie and Elaine. Thank you for all
your support and encouragement.
D.E.

PUFFIN BOOKS
UK | USA | Canada | Ireland | Australia | India | New Zealand | South Africa
Puffin Books is part of the Penguin Random House group of companies
whose addresses can be found at global.penguinrandomhouse.com.

First published 2020
002

Text copyright © Rashmi Sirdeshpande, 2020
Illustrations copyright © Diane Ewen, 2020
The moral right of the author and illustrator has been asserted
Printed and bound in Italy
A CIP catalogue record for this book is available from the British Library
ISBN: 978–0–241–39266–9

All correspondence to: Puffin Books, Penguin Random House Children's
One Embassy Gardens, New Union Square, 5 Nine Elms Lane, London SW8 5DA